THE GOSPEL OF PRIAPUS

PETER SCHUTES

The Gospel of Priapus
Copyright © 2023 by Peter Schutes Publishing.
Pulp Edition © 2024
All rights reserved.

ISBN: 978-1-963667-09-7

The story, all names, characters, and incidents portrayed in this production are fictitious. No identification with actual persons (living or deceased), places, buildings, and products is intended or should be inferred.

Cover Illustration by Duncan MacLeod

This book is for ADULT AUDIENCES ONLY. It contains substantial sexually explicit scenes with multiple partners and graphic language which may be considered offensive by some readers.

All sexual activity in this work is consensual and all sexually active characters are 18 years of age or older.

The Gospel of Priapus, adapted from imaginary ancient scrolls, contains the seeds of a cult of phallic supremacy. Following its tenets, men are free to lie with other men and generate power, potency, and the fertility of their crops. In today's modern world, this translates as wealth and influence. Heed the call of Priapus, and you will enjoy affluence, good fortune, and treasures beyond your wildest dreams.

Contus Pedalis had a legendary member. Many believe, even today, that its enormous size is a source of fertility, wealth, and virility. This simple tract houses the myth of the young man's discovery of his powers and rise to the status of a pagan god. Worshipped in the pagan world as Priapus, men established sanctuaries in his honor throughout the ancient world. Several still exist today. The cult of phallic supremacy and worship has spread even in the Americas. Through rituals of buggery and obeisance to enormous tumescent penises, crops are made more fertile, and a man's phallus becomes a source of power and prestige.

Read this legend of phallic supremacy and learn, through the bylaws in Book Two, Chapter Five, the secrets to establishing a holy place of phallic supplication. Your crops and bank accounts will grow as you submit to the hallowed sovereignty of the almighty male member. Disguised as a mere myth, this legend disseminates the secrets of wealth and prosperity. The male seed has always held properties of regeneration and growth. Even outside the womb, its reproductive powers can spawn new life for men everywhere in all aspects of their manhood.

Also available in the Anthology **Like the Greeks Do**

"Pedicare volo, tu vis decerpere poma; quod peto, si dederis, quod petis, accipies."

"I want to fuck some ass, and you want to steal some apples; if you give me what I want, you can take what you want."

— ANONYMOUS FROM THE PRIAPEIA

CONTENTS

GOSPEL OF PRIAPUS
BOOK ONE

*Being the account of Contus Pedalis and his erotic friendship
with Chrysion Bipenna, whose sacred union strengthened and
healed all who partook.*

CHAPTER 1

In Lampsacus, Hellespont, in the period of Augustus, a son was born to a family of modest means. The son was Contus Pedalis, and like the meaning of his name, he was well-endowed. The midwife mistook Contus's magnificent member as a conjoined twin.

As is common with extraordinary birth gifts, Contus's life was defined by his endowment. Word of the peculiar birth spread throughout the Hellespont and beyond. In the second week after Contus was born, three holy visitors from Anatolia arrived to see the babe. Upon seeing the peculiarly large organ, they bowed in obeisance to the infant. They told his parents that he was not an ordinary child but a demigod, born of Dionysius, who must have visited and impregnated the mother in secret. The parents of Contus agreed to let the three holy men take him to their distant temple in exchange for a small bag of gold. The mother wept but knew that her child was destined for extraordinary adventures.

So it was that Contus and his wet nurse were carried away by boat and Roman Road to Istambolia. He grew up in a temple, far from the public eye. He was raised to believe that he was divine and that the gift between his legs was his source of power. When puberty struck, his hair became black as night, and a forest sprouted at the root of his cock. He grew taller, but so did his penis lengthen so that it remained at his ankles. Its thickness doubled until it was nearly as thick as his powerful thighs, grown muscular from carrying the heavy meat.

The many holy men inhabiting the temple were swayed by the cock's power. They felt a weakness or faintness upon seeing the magnificent member. Contus grew accustomed to attention and learned to draw power from the male gaze. When he bathed, it was a holy ceremony. The men formed a circle around him and manually brought themselves to orgasm, emboldened by the mere sight of his soft penis.

One day in his eighteenth year, a dove landed on the windowsill with a Roman gold coin in its beak. It was the first time Contus had seen money.

The dove sang:

> *Shut away for none to see*
> *You reek of young virginity*
> *You hide your proud divinity*
> *The world deserves it, doesn't she?*

Contus replied, "But fair dove, I stay in this temple for my safety. I don't belong in the world. What is this strange shiny stone you bring me?"

The dove sang in reply:

> *The coin is your inheritance*
> *From parents who sold you away*

> *To holy men who profit thence*
> *And put you on display!*

Contus reeled at the news. He had only ever known the temple. The brothers told him that he had no parents, for he was born of a god. This convenient lie kept the boy prisoner all these eighteen years. To hear of a family, worse yet, a family who sold him, was painful to his ears. He said, "Fair dove, I know not the purpose of this stone. Nor what you intend I should do."

The dove sang:

> *Take the coin to travel west*
> *'Twill pay for inns to take your rest.*
> *Find Chrysion, whom fate decreed*
> *Companion for your noble quest.*

Contus said, "I know not what lies West and have not heard of an inn. Nor do I know what my quest shall be."

THE DOVE FLEW TO THE HIGHEST WINDOW AND SANG one last verse:

> *Your quest will spread your fame abroad*
> *And strengthen the divine within thee,*
> *The gods have blessed your massive rod.*
> *I will appear whene'er you need me.*

And with that, the dove flew away. The holy men of the temple came for Contus as it was bath time. He tucked the coin beneath his pillow. In the sacred bath, he stood knee-deep and washed himself as the brothers gathered the energy from his phallus with their eyes. The excitement of the quest caused a stirring in his loins that he had never felt before. He grew lightheaded as blood engorged his member. The congregation gasped as the already enormous member swelled and reached upwards. Contus himself drew his breath in astonishment at the sight of his penis swelling, lengthening, and stretching skyward. He stumbled in his bath, dropping the sponge and sitting down hard on the stone coping.

All at once, a warmth rushed through him. His mighty testicles ascended. At the place where his member joined his body, he felt a vibration as a liquid moved through the ducts. He felt faint as his member throbbed and swayed of its own accord, then released a white river that cascaded into the bath for several minutes. The surface of the bath water grew murky from the semen that issued forth from Contus. He grew fainter still; then, all was dark.

He awoke in his bed. It was evening vespers, and he could hear the brotherhood arguing fervently over the meaning of the afternoon's events.

The eldest holy man said, "He has defiled the temple with his obscene display."

Another said, "It is a miracle. Contus touched not himself and gave forth issue of a hundred men."

Yet another holy man said, "It was not known to us that it could become aroused. The prophecy said that when such a sign appeared, we should cast him from the temple."

The eldest said, "Yes, but we have nothing written in our prophecy of the ejaculation. We cannot know for certain what should be done. Perhaps we must sacrifice him to the gods."

Contus Pedalis listened to the discourse. Upon hearing of the sacrifice, he gathered his pillow, robe, and gold coin and crept outside. He dressed himself to cover the gift and climbed a peach tree by the wall. He landed on the other side and made his way into the busy port town of Istambolia.

It was still light out, for it was the summer of his eighteenth year. He heard the sound of many people speaking and a kind of music that was new to his ears. He followed this sound until he entered the bazaar. Never in his life had he seen so many people in one place. In one row, merchants displayed bright spices on cloth-covered tables. In another row, there were musical instruments. A third row had tools and locks on display.

As he walked, he saw dozens of women. He had only ever seen girls delivering goods to the men of the temple, and he wasn't allowed to gaze at them. Now seeing women of all ages with their large breasts, he grew curious. They, in turn, were curious as to what was causing his robe to billow between his legs.

One woman put out a hand to stop him. She whispered in his ear. "I can offer my cunt at a very nice price."

Not knowing what a cunt was, Contus shook his head. "I'm looking for Chrysion."

"Who?"

"I was told to find Chrysion."

The woman waved an impatient hand in the air. "There are no whores by that name here, nor are there catamites. Chrysion is a male name. Try the market by the river. There are boys for sale there."

The dove told him the coin was for an inn, not to buy a boy.

"I'm looking for an inn."

A man overheard and took him by the arm. "I am Sylvanus. My family and I run an inn. I'll make you an excellent price."

The man named Sylvanus escorted Contus through the streets of Istambolia until he arrived near the waterfront at a large house with many rooms.

When Sylvanus demanded payment, Contus presented the gold coin.

"Son, that will pay for several years at this inn! I can't take your money. But I could not but notice on our walk here that you are blessed beyond all belief. If I may but see what springs from your loins, I will grant you a week's stay."

So Contus lifted his robe. Sylvanus grew weak and sat down hard. He stayed seated, searching for air, for several minutes. When at last, his breath returned, he stood. "Come, let me show you your room."

CHAPTER 2

The following day, after a generous morning meal, Sylvanus gave Contus directions to the boy market on the Bosphorus. Contus followed the water until he reached a large bazaar much like the one from the previous night. But this was different. There were no women or spices at this market. There were tools, leather garments, swords, and weapons, and many adolescent boys in various states of undress. Catamites.

A tall, virile boy approached him. "Two Lira for a visit to paradise."

Contus asked, "Are you Chrysion?"

The boy spat. "No, I'm Abel. Chrysion? What do you want with that piece of trash?"

Contus smiled. "You know Chrysion?"

The genuine innocence of Contus disarmed the boy. His scowl changed to a smile. "I know him. Hey Chrysion!"

From the long row of boys emerged a gentle, fair-haired youth. He opened his arms and came towards them.

"Are you Contus? The dove told me you would come!" His eyes strayed below Contus's belt. "Yes, you must be he, for I was told of your enormous blessing."

Abel looked down and whistled. "Gods, you're enormous! You could make much money with that!"

Chrysion took Contus by the hand. "We are to return to your inn, where I will lay with you."

Abel laughed. "He shall surely kill you if you lay together."

Contus frowned. "I have no desire to kill Chrysion."

Abel shrugged. "You don't understand me. But no matter. I have work to do."

Chrysion held hands with Contus as they retraced his steps along the water. When they got to the inn, Sylvanus greeted them.

"If you wish to have a guest, I will need to touch it."

Contus agreed. Sylvanus got on the ground and put his hand on the end of the massive pole. He stood, feeling the length until he reached the spot where cock and testicles attached to his crotch. He perspired and panted but remained standing, holding the flesh as heavy as a bag of stones.

"Welcome to the Inn."

Upstairs, Contus removed his robe. Chrysion's face showed fear.

"What is it?"

"The dove said I should lay with you, but I am frightened because it is too much of a blessing."

Contus was a virgin, and he had no notion what could be wrong with lying down beside him. "It is big, but there's room for you on my bed."

Chrysion laughed. The dove said you were pure, and I see what he meant. I mean to lay with you.

Contus was still terribly confused. Chrysion removed his robes, revealing his secret. He had a very large posterior but almost nothing in front. Contus had never seen such a small penis. The holy men were of many sizes but none so tiny as Chrysion; seeing it aroused him.

Chrysion stood pressed against the wall as the massive cock swelled and stretched upwards. Feeling faint, Contus sat on the bed. He had only just discovered this strange ability to grow and stretch, and it was upon him again without any way to control it.

Chrysion knelt in worship before the great phallus. He wrapped his arms around it, hugging it to his bare chest. With his tongue, he traced long lines up the shaft. He had to stand to reach the head, which resembled a large, red apple. He put his mouth on it and licked the slit, already flowing with clear semen. His tiny penis throbbed against the giant.

Contus had never been touched this way. The act of worship was familiar to him but only as an object to be gazed upon from afar. This act was a more profound communion, a uniting of his soul to Chrysion's. To be embraced by such a beautiful boy with such a perfect, tiny penis was holy.

Chrysion grew aware of the sacredness of their act. He had lain with many men, but none like Contus. Holding the massive phallus in his arms, licking and kissing the head, gave his mind clarity of purpose. He would consume the holy seed when it came.

Contus's breath grew more rapid. The sensation in his loins grew more intense. He felt bolts of lightning where Chrysion's tiny penis connected with his. A roaring thunder followed the lightning in his testicles. His body shook. Chrysion stroked the shaft, pushing Contus over a precipice. He ejaculated.

Chrysion swallowed over and over again, barely able to keep up with the cups of ejaculate that flowed from Contus's loins. He refused to waste a drop. When it was over, he had eaten enough to feed him for a day and night.

And so the first ceremony of Phallic worship was born; it became the guiding light for both young men. But a deeper communion was required before they could begin the quest.

CHAPTER 3

The next day, the two companions returned to the market where they met. Chrysion had a pouch of lead coins, the common currency in Istambolia. He purchased an ointment made of butter, lavender, and herbs from Babylonia with one coin. When rubbed on the skin, it reduces sensation. Chrysion had used this when he lay with men whose members were very large. It might help him manage the colossal task ahead.

On the road back to the inn, three men with dark souls stopped them. One wielded a scimitar and demanded their money—the other two held daggers to their throats. Chrysion handed over his bag of lead coins, and Contus had to surrender his gold coin, his inheritance. The men were about to cut their throats when a horse-drawn carriage passed by. Fearing someone might spot them, the three thieves ran. Contus ran down many streets in pursuit of the men. They entered a tavern, and Contus followed them in.

The man with the scimitar spun around as if to run him through. Contus side-stepped the sword and grabbed the man by the throat. With his other hand, he wielded his cock and slammed it into the man's head, rendering him unconscious. The two men with knives came forward. When Contus swung his huge cock at one of them, he tried to stab it. But the blade broke, and the colossal cock hit him in the throat. The man fell to the ground gasping for air. The third man held the money out, and Contus took it. The man tried to stab his hand, but Contus swung his massive penis and hit the man in the stomach. He doubled over and collapsed.

When Contus left the tavern, he realized he was lost. He found the waterfront and walked in the direction that should lead him to the boy market. But he was turned around and grew even more lost. He sat on the river bank and wept. He had never been lost before, having lived his entire life in the temple. He was afraid he would never find his companion or the inn. He looked to the sky and cried, "I am lost."

The dove who had brought him the coin landed beside him.

The dove sang:

> *In woods or city be ye lost*
> *Find the sun at any cost*
> *Follow the shadow to the inn*
> *Where Chrysion awaits within.*
>
> *And though you wish to start your quest*
> *To find your fortune in the West*
> *Your pole must enter Chrysion first*
> *Though pain ye cause, he will not burst*

Then she flew away. Contus followed the flight of the bird as it crossed the sun. He covered his eyes against the blinding rays. There was a massive temple with a tower that reached for the sky. The structure cast long shadows across the tops of houses for several blocks. Contus followed the shadow, and just as the dove promised, there was the inn. Chrysion was up in the room waiting for him.

"Did you retrieve the gold?"

Contus nodded. "And the lead, too."

Chrysion said, "But you have no weapon."

The strapping youth laughed. "But I do, Chrysion. I have a club so strong it will knock a man senseless." He grabbed his member for emphasis. "It cannot be cut by knife or sword, for it is holy."

Chrysion said, "I doubt it not, for you grow hard as chestnut when aroused. You carry a heavy club between your legs."

"I saw the dove today," said Contus, "He sang that I must enter you. What does it mean? I see no doorway."

Chrysion bent forward and parted his buttocks, revealing a cavernous hole. "Many men have lain with me. The balm of Gilead shall ease your entry into my hole."

The sight of the wide, dark hole caused Contus to swell quickly. He lost his balance and sat on the bed. Chrysion pushed Contus by the shoulders until he lay flat, the tower of flesh reaching high above him. He applied the balm liberally to his hole until it was greased and numb. Standing on the tips of his toes, Chrysion guided the apple-sized head to the entry. He pressed down until his buttocks parted, allowing the very end to enter. There it lodged, unable to continue.

Contus said, "I have entered you!"

Chrysion shook his head. "Nay, 'tis but the tip."

"But it feels good."

Chrysion smiled. "It is not enough. Keep pressing, and you will know pleasure unlike any other." Determined, the fair youth lifted his legs until he sat upon the flesh as though it were a tavern stool. Of a sudden, his hole gave way, admitting the whole apple at once.

Contus widened his eyes. "Gods, what is this feeling? Your buttocks embrace me!"

The youth nodded. "And you shall feel the full embrace if you are patient and temperate. Spill not your seed yet." Putting his full weight, the youth filled the first chamber with Contus's mighty flesh. As he learned in his trade, he leaned to one side, allowing the meat hammer to invade the second chamber. With much pressing and twisting, he filled the second chamber to the end. His eyes flapped like the wings of a butterfly.

Contus frowned. "I'm hurting you."

Chrysion nodded. "But it is a sweet pain." The second chamber was filled. When the mighty cock came in contact with the third chamber, Chrysion felt a holy union. In waves, his insides danced across Contus's staff. The cock was halfway in now.

The waves of holy spasms left Contus breathless. "I am close to spilling my seed."

Chrysion shook his head. "There's more. Refrain. Think of something else."

Contus thought of the woman in the bazaar, which distracted him from the intense pleasure that threatened to push him over the precipice. Chrysion grabbed the remaining flesh and pulled it inside him. The third chamber filled rapidly, stretching the boy's insides. It was a much longer chamber than the other two, and it accommodated the entirety of Contus. He sat on his knees, letting his buttocks come to rest on Contus's lap. He rocked up and down, stroking the holy monster with his insides.

"Gods, Chrysion, I fear I will not last long."

The boy nodded. "If you cannot wait, I am ready."

Contus grabbed the boy, pulling him down hard. The youth's eyes grew wide.

Chrysion said, "Oh! Bliss. Sweet Bliss." His tiny penis throbbed before it flowed with his seed, basting the face of Contus.

The larger youth was astonished. He tasted the sweet seed and closed his eyes. At that moment, he reached the summit.

"It is coming. The moment is here!" He groaned with pleasure as his giant testicles released their seed. He poured buckets inside Chrysion. The warm fluid filled the tight chamber, and when it had nowhere to go, the walls stretched even further. All the while, the spasms squeezed and nursed Contus's tremendous cock.

"I'll burst!" Chrysion pounded his fist on his lover's chest.

But there was no stopping the river. The seed pushed through into the fourth chamber. Chrysion breathed a sigh of relief. "Oh, Contus, I believe I love you."

Contus heard the words but was in the throes of holy communion with his lover. The spasms grew more intense, milking his great udder until it released more seed. He trembled with pleasure.

Then the spasms grew painful. Even as Contus softened, he still stretched Chrysion wide. Chrysion's body struggled to expel the great beast and the tide of seed behind it. The boy rose on his knees, but the great colossus remained wedged between the second and third chambers. Carefully he rose until, at last, the apple popped into the second chamber, then the first, each time making the sound of hands clapping. With force, Chrysion pushed the apple from the first chamber, clamping tight to hold the seed inside.

"Where is my issue?"

"It remains inside me; I cannot keep it long. My bowels yearn to expel it."

"It should not go to waste." Contus took the wash basin from the bedside table and held it under his lover's clenched anus. With a sigh of relief, Chrysius opened his hole, filling the wash basin with the holy seed.

Contus said, "This is my body and my blood. We shall drink of it."

They took turns taking large gulps from the basin until it was all gone. It satisfied not just physical hunger but spiritual thirst as well. The longing for connection to the divine was fulfilled by drinking the sacred issue of Contus's loins. It was communion.

When Chrysion bent to retrieve his tunic, Contus marveled at the abyss between his buttocks. "I made that," he thought. Without a questioning thought further, he leaned forward and licked the rim of the gaping hole. There he found more seed and was nourished.

He followed a line of semen down one thigh. Where

yesterday had been only soft boy flesh, today there were sinews. The buttocks were slightly more firm, and he saw cords of muscle beneath the soft belly fat.

"Chrysion, you have grown muscle."

The boy felt his abdomen, and indeed it was hard beneath the layer of fat. "It can only be a miracle of the holy seed."

Contus had tasted of the seed this day. He wondered if he, too, should sprout muscle or if his own body was immune to the healing properties.

"Shall we head West?"

"I should like to stay in bed with you a fortnight, but tomorrow we can leave."

They did not need supper. Chrysion lay nestled in Contus's arms, and they fell asleep in that loving embrace that resembles two spoons.

Contus awoke in the night to feel Chrysion's hand on his cock. The youth lay on his side, guiding the soft beast to his hole. With ease, he engulfed the soft head. As he backed into the giant, it swelled of its own accord. It reached the third chamber but could not pass further until fully engorged. As it grew, it climbed into the third chamber of its own accord. In this position, Contus could swivel his hips, pushing and pulling the great meat through the entrails of Chrysion. With the motion, the fair youth began to tremor and quake inside.

"Oh gods, Contus. You have made a vessel of me!"

The demigod imagined an amphora of olive oil, which hastened the production of pre-ejaculate, causing Chrysion's insides to become lubricated. The pushing and pulling grew less of a chore and more of a delight. It had the same effect on Chrysion, whose eyes disappeared into his forehead as he emitted a loud moan.

Contus grew confident that he wouldn't destroy the boy. He increased the pace, making loud clapping sounds as he entered and exited the third chamber. He lengthened his strokes, creating a clapping twice as he exited and re-entered the second and third chambers. With each clap, Chrysion shuddered in ecstasy. Once in the shape of a large 'S,' his innards had become a letter 'C.' They were rearranged to suit the needs of the god cock. Contus was grateful that Chrysion had cleared a pathway for him to enter heaven.

The light-haired youth shook involuntarily as the mighty cock brought his body into orgasm. His tiny penis followed, scattering seed on the floor of the room.

Contus was not finished. He had learned to withhold his seed and prolong his pleasure. Each in-stroke embraced his member in warm flesh, and each out-stroke held it, begging it not to leave.

Chrysion did not soften. His small penis throbbed anew. It was not from touching himself that he ejaculated again, but this time he caught the semen in his hand and fed it to Contus.

The black-haired god devoured the semen, as sweet and satisfying as his own. The taste remained on his tongue, reminding him of the great feast he produced between his own legs. The tingling on his tongue sent him over the precipice. In long, brutal strokes, he finished his work inside Chrysion, releasing a banquet of semen deep in his gut.

Together they caught the feast in the wash basin and consumed it.

Chrysion said, "Tomorrow, I shall grow strong as Hercules."

Contus nodded. "And I shall have two breasts like dinner plates."

The fair-haired lover laughed. "Forsooth, we shall have a vessel to dine on your semen."

Contus said, "I shall serve you nightly. Bring a spoon."

Then the exhausted lovers made two spoons and slept.

CHAPTER 4

In the morning, Chrysion said, "Contus, I fear my vessel is closing. I need you to open it again."

It was true. The ease with which Contus had entered the night before was gone. He applied the salve liberally to the hole, which had returned to its former state. With his fingers, he spread the tight valve until it was pliable. Chrysion knelt on the bed, his posterior aimed at his lover.

Contus grew aroused at the sight of his supine companion, and as he swelled, he put the apple-sized head inside. With some force, he entered the second chamber. At the third chamber opening, he met with great resistance.

"Chrysion, can you spare me entrance?"

The boy shook his head. "It is your task to open the gates; I have no power over them."

Stretching his arms, Contus was able to grasp his waist. With force, he pulled the fair youth to him. The mighty god cock penetrated the third chamber and easily slid upwards to fill it.

Chrysion cried in pain. His insides were learning to accept the holy penis, but the change was painful.

Contus asked, "Are you hurt? Should I stop?"

Chrysion shook his head. "It is a good pain that turns to pleasure. Please continue."

Contus felt his pubic hairs brush against the boy's buttocks; he was all the way inside.

Holding Chrysion by the waist, he pulled back as far as his arms allowed, then pushed forward, holding the boy to keep him from falling off the edge of the bed.

"Ohh! Ow! Ohh!" Chrysion wavered between pleasure and pain.

Contus found a rhythm and kept it like the regular beat of a large drum at ceremonies. The double claps kept time as he plunged in and out of the inner chambers.

"Ohh! Yes! Yes!" The pain gave way to ecstatic bliss. Chrysion trembled and quaked inside.

Contus had cleared the path again so that his penetration required less effort. He leaned over his lover and held his shoulders, his powerful chest resting on the boy's muscular back. Instinctively, he kissed Chrysion's neck.

He whispered in his ear. "I should like to do this with you for all eternity."

The boy couldn't answer; he was too deep in blissful union. He made animal grunts instead. He held his torso aloft with both hands; he could neither touch himself nor his lover. But in the short time they were together, Contus had learned when Chrysion was about to ejaculate. It was a subtle quickening of the breath and a tightening of the anus. He put one giant hand down there and caught the seed, which they shared, sipping from his cupped hand.

The elixir again had the potent property of pushing Contus past the brink of orgasm. Holding Chrysion by the neck and hair, he drove his seed deep inside the boy. As was befitting the god of cock, Contus never had a small ejaculation, and every time it was enough to fill a wash basin.

Chrysion squatted over the large bowl and released the holy milk. Together, the god and the boy took turns feeding on the semen until it was gone. They were full and satisfied.

Chrysion said, "I know now you are a god, for my insides are healed of every wound by your seed."

Contus blushed. "I am a mortal. I was born of man."

The fair-haired boy said, "The gods can plant seeds in mortals and produce more gods."

The darker boy said, "If that's true, then have I planted a god in you?"

Chrysion burst into laughter. "Had I a womb, I fear you may have planted a god in me. But I am content to worship your god-given gift. You may plant all you wish, for I am the happier to accommodate such greatness."

CHAPTER 5

It was still early. The two lovers, one mortal and the other a god, left Istambolia on their mysterious quest. They took the road in the direction of the shadows, heading West towards Thrace.

They passed merchants, beggars, soldiers, and politicians on the great Roman road. Many gasped in astonishment, for they could see the outline of Contus's mighty cock through the fabric of his robe. But none stopped to speak. It was a well-worn, passable road connecting Asia Minor to the Northern Roman Empire. Their feet grew tired after many thousands of steps. They saw the lights of a small town on the horizon. There they would stay at an inn and continue their rites of the worship of cock.

The inn was small and humble. The owner asked for only one lead coin for a night's stay, which included wine, bread, and oil for dipping. Having eaten nothing all day, the two were grateful for the meal. The wine was strong; the two became drunk. They ascended to their room, tasting each other's mouths and lips. With haste, they removed their garments and began the worship of the phallus. Chrysion kissed the tip, licked it, rubbed it, and watched as it doubled in size, then tripled. Letting go of the massive beast, he bent to remove his sandals. As he stood, Contus swiveled and accidentally clubbed him. The boy fell unconscious.

Chrysion awoke in the morning with a terrible headache and a bump on his forehead. Contus wrung his hands worriedly, not noticing that Chrysion was awake.

The boy spoke. "You wield a powerful club, friend. It's your lightning bolt of Zeus or your spear of Pallas Athena."

Contus rushed to his side. "Are you well? I feared I may have killed you, for you wouldn't wake."

Chrysion smiled weakly. "I am fine, but my head aches."

"Mine too. The wine was not pure, I fear."

"We must worship, and in so doing, will gain the elixir to bolster our strength for the road."

And so the two nourished one another with their seed, and their heads ceased to ache.

"The communion of seed is good," said Chrysion, "for it gives us strength and heals our ailments. We must share the good news, for you are a great physician of the gods."

In the tavern downstairs, a large, swarthy man wept into his cup of wine.

Contus put a hand on his shoulder. "What brings you sorrow, brother?"

The man lifted his head, wiping tears from his red eyes. "I am a wrestler, but I suffered an injury yesterday and now am lame."

He pointed to his leg, which bore a splint. "I can no longer earn my keep."

Chrysion spoke. "Fortune has brought you to us. We have only just learned of our healing powers and seek to share them with the world. Care you for a cure?"

The wrestler frowned. "I can scarce afford the ointment or draft you are peddling."

"We give it freely, for it costs us nothing to make."

"Then there is naught to lose. How do you cure me?"

Contus said, "Come upstairs to our room, and we will heal you."

The wrestler pointed to his leg. "I can no longer climb stairs. I stay in the manger. Can you perform the miracle there?"

The two lovers nodded. Together they helped the powerful wrestler to his feet. With one arm around each boy, he hopped outside to the barn where he slept.

Chrysion whispered to Contus. "I doubt you should try to enter him. He appears to be an active lover, not a catamite."

Contus nodded. He said, "O Dove, how can I heal this man?"

The dove flew down from the rafters and sang:

> *Contus puts the cock of god*
> *In Chrysion, the physician*
> *The patient joins the mighty rod*
> *Thus mingling their emission*
>
> *Chrysion's seed shall stitch the flesh.*
> *And Contus mend the bone.*
> *But patient's seed shall seal the scroll*
> *Communion shall be known*
>
> *And when at last communion ends.*
> *The patient, too, can heal.*
> *For you have passed the gift to friends*
> *Through semen's sacred seal*

And the dove flew out of the barn into the bright morning sky.

With that explanation, the healing duo knew they must become a trio to heal the wrestler.

"I am Contus, and this is Chrysion. What is your name, sir?"

"I am Dyemuya, the legendary wrestler. Have you heard of me?"

Chrysion said, "Yes. I have seen that name on posters in Istambolia. You are famous."

The wrestler grinned. "I am. But have you not heard of me, Contus?"

Chrysion answered for him. "Only a few days ago, he had been cloistered in a temple his entire life. He had no opportunity to know of your greatness."

Dyemuya chuckled and grabbed his bulging crotch. "Greatness indeed."

The wrestler, overflowing with confidence, had only looked Contus in the eyes. Having spoken of his own penis, he did as all men do and looked at the others. Chrysion revealed nothing, of course, but when he saw the serpent between Contus's legs, he started. "Gods, but you're blessed!" His gaze continued downward. "Is that your cock I spy at your ankles?"

Contus nodded and smiled. "Fear not, though our cure requires seed, I will not enter your sacred pathway. Together you and I will fill Chrysion with our seed."

The wrestler looked doubtful. "How is that possible? You surpass a horse in girth and stature."

Chrysion spoke. "I am a vessel for his seed. As much as he is gifted in size, so too am I blessed internally with depth.

The talk had aroused the wrestler, whose prick reached skyward. By any mortal account, it was massive, but it was nothing compared to the god cock of Contus.

Dyemuya lay on his back on the soft hay, his legs open wide and his cock standing straight up into the sky, more than half a cubit in length. It was as big around as it was long. Chrysion sat upon it. As quickly as a baby takes a breath, he inhaled the giant cock until it came to rest in the second chamber.

The wrestler commented. "When I lay with catamites, I often hear them scream. You offered no resistance."

Contus stood between the wrestler's legs. "That's because he has grown accustomed to my holy member."

The wrestler had seen it through his robe, but he trembled now that it was exposed. "It's so powerful; I felt it in my heart. It's magnificent to behold."

Contus nodded. "You can draw power by gazing upon it, but this will heal you."

Carefully, Contus pressed the head of his cock to Chrysion's opening. As though the gods themselves willed it, he entered him with little force. The power of his cock rubbed off onto the wrestler's cock. Easily he passed out of the first chamber, past the end of Dyemuya's cock, and into the third chamber.

The wrestler was fascinated by the large round buttocks on Chrysion. He rubbed them as Contus did the hard work, sliding betwixt the walls and the wrestler's massive cock.

As he was wont to do, Chrysion began to spasm inside.

"Oh, Apollo and Aphrodite, what is that?" The wrestler's eyes opened wide. "I feel as though a hand were inside you, stroking me!"

Chrysion said, "That is the beginning of the healing process." Then his eyes looked skyward until they were inside his forehead, and he knew bliss.

Contus knew that the more ferociously he fucked, the stronger the medicine. With savagery, he impaled Chrysion repeatedly, building heat and friction against the wrestler's long, thick cock. All three men had passed into an ecstatic communion. There were no words, only animal sounds.

Chrysion's breath grew shallow, signaling the imminent release of his seed. Contus put the wrestler's meaty paw in the path of Chrysion's tiny penis so that he caught all the seed as it sprayed forth.

Silently, with great reverence, the wrestler sipped the precious fluid before passing it to Contus, then

Chrysion himself. He circulated it a second time until his hand was licked clean.

In the brief time it took for the trio to lap up the holy fluid, Chrysion again took many light breaths. This time the wrestler raised his hand unaided and caught the second helping of semen, which was even more than the first. As they sipped, Dyemuya reached the summit.

"I've arrived. Here it comes." All three men felt the hot blast of fluid that coated Contus's cock and lubricated Chrysion's insides.

Contus slowed his furious pounding, then held himself all the way inside his lover as his hot semen flooded the third chamber and leaked into the fourth. The barn was silent but for the heavy breaths of the three men. They stayed locked together for several minutes, enjoying the manly exchange of energy.

At last, Dyemuya softened and slipped out of the hole. Contus carefully withdrew so as not to spill his holy seed nor the wrestler's sacred semen. In a milk pail, Chrysion emptied his bowels of the precious fluids. The wrestler marveled at the enormous quantity of semen.

"Mine is but a fraction."

Contus nodded. "I think it's enough. Drink."

Dyemuya drank freely from the milk bucket. He wiped his lips with his wrist and passed it to Chrysion, who drank enough to satisfy. Contus drank much, too. The milk pail was still full. They passed around the bucket repeatedly, growing drunk on sperm. Dyemuya took the last swallow and burped.

"I'm so full; I may never eat again."

The three men lay in the hay, looking at the barn rafters.

The wrestler broke the silence. "How long does it take?"

Chrysion said, "You're our first patient, and we have

only tasted of the healing seed ourselves. But it worked fast when I was sore inside."

Dyemuya lifted his leg and moved it. "There is pain, but it is much less."

Contus said, "My seed is knitting your leg bone back together."

Chrysion said, "And where the bone has broken through the flesh, you will see the skin has healed."

Dyemuya drew up his tunic and found only a faint scar. He loosened the splint and removed it. His knee bent and straightened.

"This is a miracle. I must pay you!"

Contus shook his head. "It costs us nothing."

"But it's the work of the gods themselves. Surely you put a price on that!"

Contus stroked his chin. "Spread the good news. Tell them of the holy seed. Share your seed; for now, it is imbued with healing powers, too."

Dyemuya wept, but now it was for joy, not self-pity. "I have the healing power, too?"

Contus nodded. A little bird told me so.

CHAPTER 6

Dyemuya had a horse and cart. The lovers could heal the day's blisters with communion, but the wrestler was traveling west on the road anyway. They accepted his offer of a ride to Thrace.

"In Uskudama, I will wrestle in the competition, and I often win, despite not being as powerful as the other wrestlers. Do you know my secret?"

Chrysion shook his head.

"This." He pointed to his cock.

Contus said, "I don't understand."

Dyemuya grinned proudly. "I am much, much bigger than the other wrestlers down there. Many of them are hung like Chrysion...no offense."

"None taken"

Contus shrugged. "I still don't get it."

The wrestler gave a wink. "We wrestle without clothes. Not only does my superiority give me advantage over their mind, but there is also a rule that disqualifies anyone touching another wrestler's cock with their hand."

The three travelers laughed heartily.

Dyemuya said, "Hey, imagine if you wrestled, Contus? You're strong enough, and you wouldn't surpass thirty seconds before your opponent was out of the match."

Contus smiled. "I don't know that it would further my mission."

Chrysion interjected. "It would be a way of spreading the good news. By exposing your member to spectators, your fame would spread, and so too the knowledge of your healing. You could act as physician to the wrestlers."

Contus sat up straight. Chrysion was right. There were many athletes in need of his healing powers. But what if they were too small to share in communion? How would he heal them then?

THE DOVE LANDED ON THE EDGE OF THE CART AND sang:

> *The small shall gain your healing too*
> *They stand before your face*
> *You drink from them their tiny spew*
> *And thus impart your grace.*

And away flew the dove as quickly as she'd arrived.

The road to Uskudama was four days' travel by cart, so the three shared rooms at inns along the route. They avoided the wine, which was terrible in that region.

When Chrysion broke bread, his biceps bulged. A few days earlier, his arms were soft and weak.

Contus said, "My seed has made you strong, friend."

Chrysion grinned. "I have never felt such power."

Dyemuya, the wrestler, listened intently. "You say you had no muscles before?"

Chrysion shook his head. "I was a boy less than a week ago, and I'm now a man. My chest has sprouted thick hairs, and my beard is growing in.

The wrestler blushed and said, "I should like to partake of communion once again, that my leg grows stronger."

Contus agreed. In the room, when the three travelers had filled their basin and drank their fill, Chrysion flexed his muscles. He was no longer shaped like a pear but an inverted triangle atop two powerful legs. His penis did not grow. His power came from the tiny member. He was happy, for as a catamite, men revered his small penis as beautiful. He never wanted it to change.

Dyemuya, however, would gain power in wrestling with the growth of his member. His desire to grow bigger mingled with the communion seed. On the third night, when he checked, it had grown closer to his knee. He was nearly two-thirds of a cubit now in length and girth. He flexed an arm and stared in amazement at his massive bicep. His chest had grown more pronounced so that his nipples pointed downwards on the hillocks of his breast.

Late the following evening, they arrived in Uskudama. Dyemuya drove the cart to the wrestling arena. It was little more than a square patch of grass with many wooden seats on risers. Adjacent to the wrestling green was a large building housing the local wrestlers and any visitors. Dyemuya spoke with the owners of the building and secured two rooms.

"We can stay here for free, but there's a wrestler

who cannot move his legs, and he has paralysis. Can you share communion with him?"

Contus nodded. "Take me to him."

The injured wrestler, Koipides, sat in a chair with carriage wheels. He traveled by means of his arms.

Dyemuya asked, "Are you in pain, brother?"

Koipides said, "I feel no pain, which I fear is worse. I cannot move my legs. Perhaps a witch has hexed me."

Contus touched the legs made soft by immobility. He put a hand on the man's penis.

Koipides turned his head sharply. "I feel that, sir. What do you intend?"

It was not a large penis, nor was it small. But it was soft. Contus said, "I need to manipulate it to see if you can grow."

The man said, "Certainly, I can grow. Not like Dyemuya, but I am larger than many."

Contus determined that it would not pass into the second chamber and was, therefore, not suitable for the communion of twin penetration. He would have to try the second method.

"You will find my healing method pleasant but strange. If you doubt, know that Dyemuya was lame four days hitherto."

Koipides agreed to the peculiar ritual, despite feeling distaste for union with men. If it restored his withered legs, he would do anything.

The coordination to achieve this communion was made more difficult by Koipides's inability to stand with his cock at mouth level. Contus was perplexed, but Chrysion, having worked as a catamite for many years, was an expert in complex arrangements. He lay face down on the bed, and Contus lay perpendicular, forming a cross, entering from the side. His head rested in the patient's lap, allowing him to take communion directly from the penis.

Because the injury was so severe, Dyemuya offered

to give communion directly to Koipides. In this way, the healing energies would multiply.

The crippled man sucked seed from Dyemuya, drank Chrysion's sweet boy seed, and consumed large helpings of Contus's holy seed gathered from the anus of Chrysion. He was the last to give his seed, for his loins were much impaired. When the communion issued forth, his toes curled. Contus kissed each man, sharing the seed of the cripple with them. Koipides gave a gasp of surprise when his legs twitched.

"I feel my toes! I feel my legs!"

After several more days of these complicated communions, Koipides rose from his chair and walked. The news traveled quickly among the athletes. A holy man, a healer, walked among them.

CHAPTER 7

Contus trained with Dyemuya for the competition. First, they stripped off their clothing. Next, they doused each other in olive oil to make their bodies slick. With a judge on hand to oversee their trials, they wrestled. Over and over, Dyemuya was disqualified, as his hands couldn't avoid touching the colossal cock. As long as both men concentrated on areas above the waist, they remained in the match. But the match could never end with a navel pointed skyward without a move below the waist. Many matches lasted hours while the two men grappled, penises touching, causing arousal.

There was no rule against one man's penis in contact with the other, so they did it often, despite the ensuing erections. Once they were both erect, with cocks pointed skyward, they could reach below the waist. There were no rules against ears or faces touching penises, only hands. So they found they could only wrestle when fully erect. The judge was certain there should be a rule against wrestling in this condition, especially with two men so greatly endowed (for now, Dyemuya's penis was a full cubit in length and three-fourths in girth). But only a committee could rewrite the rule book, so the men entered the match as opponents.

On the day of the fight, Chrysion oiled up both men, taking extra care to rub oil into the deep folds of the two massive penises. He rubbed until both men were aroused and kept them in a constant state of arousal until the announcer called their match.

The spectators were astonished by the massive cocks. No matter that Contus dwarfed Dyemuya, they were both large enough to be seen in the highest riser. Wrestling entirely below the waist, if one man became soft, it would lie on the shoulder of the opponent, who would use his ear or forehead to stimulate the opponent back to full arousal. In this way, the far more experienced man won the match. Contus lay belly up, cock covering his face. The crowd roared.

Dyemuya wrestled until he reached the final match. In every fight, he could defeat his challenger by skill and by reason of his enormous cock. At the contest's climax, Dyemuya was the champion because the reigning champion touched his huge member and thereby lost the crown.

As the contest disbanded, well-wishers and the curious came to speak with the two men. Many touched the great god-phallus or stroked the lesser of the two.

Arslan, A local patrician, invited Dyemuya and Contus to his home in the hills above Uskudama. He promised figs from Africa, spices from the Indus, and meats from the forests of Dacia.

Dyemuya thought quickly. "Only if each can bring a guest."

The patrician waved his hand. "But of course. Bring who you like."

Dyemuya brought Koipides, who had regained his

strength and grew more robust than before the fall. Contus brought his fair-haired lover. The four were all healers now, for they had partaken in communion, and the sacred seed of Contus Pedalis coursed through their veins.

Arslan took no wife. He lived with Gyorgi, a boy lover who served him with great devotion. As promised, the table overflowed with delicacies from throughout the Roman Empire. As the men ate, a band played haunting melodies on horns, flutes, and drums. The music was as intoxicating as the wine from Etruria. The mirth and merriment gave way to confessions of lust.

Gyorgi said, "Dyemuya, I have longed for your cock inside me since I first attended a match many years ago. Now it is so big that my desire has multiplied a hundredfold."

Dyemuya stood and removed his tunic. "Come to me, boy, and take what you will."

Gyorgi disrobed, revealing a diminutive penis much like Chrysion's, but not as pretty and not as small. Dyemuya dropped to his knees and buried his nose in the boy's posterior, making it wet and slippery with saliva.

Arslan gestured to Koipides. The athlete came to the patrician's side, and they kissed. Koipides had grown in length and girth as a side effect of the communion. The patrician stroked it but surprised him by revealing a regal cock rivaling Koipides's in size and strength. A four-way union was formed, with Dyemuya inside Gyorgi, Arslan inside Koipides, and Gyorgi taking direct communion from the cock of Koipides.

Contus held Chrysion's hand. "We have formed the first church of the sacred seed. These men will not waste a drop; all will partake of the holy communion. The healer's gift will pass to these two new men, and the church will grow.

Chrysion said, "I wish to take private communion with you."

Contus emptied a fruit bowl, then brought his lover to the balcony overlooking Uskudama, Orestia, and the confluence of the Tonzos and Evros rivers. Chrysion stood at the railing and bent, so his gaping anus was accessible. Contus walked forward until the apple was against the peach. He met very little resistance as he stepped closer. Chrysion's entrails were accustomed to the invasion and welcomed him warmly. His moans were not cries of pain; they were howls of ecstasy. Every moment his lover was inside him was a glimpse of paradise on Earth. He was in the garden of delights, swallowing the apple whole. In just these few days, Contus had surpassed the skills of any client Chrysion had served. Because the gods created his phallus, it was only fitting that they should have blessed him with an extraordinary natural skill in the sexual arts. What better teacher than the highly skilled catamite, Chrysion?

With the fat layer gone, Chrysion's abdomen revealed the outline of Contus's cock on its path in and out of the third chamber. Chrysion put a hand on his belly and squeezed, pinching the giant cock between his fingers.

Contus shuddered at the new sensation. The fair-haired youth's insides began to spasm. The waves of peristalsis massaged his member and hugged it from the inside. As before, Chrysion's breath grew rapid and shallow. Contus put a hand below and caught the effluence. He fed it to his boy before lapping up the remaining sweet nectar.

They were so tuned to the signals of each other's bodies that they could anticipate each progression. Chrysion felt the enormous cock grow more slippery as the clear seed lubricated his passageway. He knew it would be soon that Contus climaxed. This knowledge aroused him, and his breath grew shallow once more. Again, he spilled his seed into his lover's hand, and they both partook.

Contus took shorter and shorter strokes, a sure sign that Chrysion's entrails would soon fill. "I'm here." He flooded the boy with his sacred communion, the body, and the blood. He held Chrysion's head close to his and kissed him while the endless flow of semen continued. Each time they did it alone, the flow was more. They had produced too much. Chrysion squatted and filled the fruit bowl almost to the top. They took large gulps, but they wouldn't finish. They brought it to the orgy in the dining room and fed it to the four men and the three musicians.

Arslan stretched out his hand. "I have suffered from arthritis for ten years, and now I can stretch my hand. What is this miracle?"

Chrysion and Contus explained the miracle of the holy seminal communion. Arslan listened closely.

"I shall build a church right here in Uskudama and consecrate it to the healing of physical ailments."

And so the first Temple of Phallic Worship was born.

GOSPEL OF PRIAPUS
BOOK TWO

Being the account of the travels of Chrysion Bipenna and Contus Pedalis to the Macedonian city of Thessaloniki, where they meet Kolossos, discover the fertility embodied in the seed of Contus, and the Temple of Praiapus receives its name.

CHAPTER 1

After seven seasons of wrestling, the dove appeared again to Contus and Chrysion. It sang:

> *A single church shall grow in time*
> *But time is up; the clock will chime*
> *Faster will the church be spread*
> *If you but travel where you're led.*

With much sadness, the duo announced to the church, which had grown to thirty members, that they must depart to form new churches abroad. The athlete Dyemuya, whose member had swollen to an impressive size exceeding a cubit, was ordained as the church's first minister, so Contus was free to depart. Many boyish men with tiny penises like Chrysion's could fulfill the role, but Gyorgi was appointed high priest because he was the first to give sweet seed without Chrysion present.

Arslan provided them with a heavy bag of silver and a horse and cart with wheels calibrated for the Roman Road to Athina. The wheels fit perfectly in the ruts.

CHAPTER 2

On a warm day in Autumn, they departed, taking the southwest road in the direction of Macedonia and Achaia. The distance was nearly 600 miles. They could cover 80 miles in a day or 100 if they started early and finished late. But they found the horse couldn't go more than 75 miles a day, so they were obliged to stay in several different inns in towns and cities along the Macedonian coast. The road was not always smooth. A wheel came off the wagon outside the metropolis of Thessaloniki. The two men gathered their most essential belongings and abandoned the cart. Although they had no saddle, they could fashion saddlebags out of large blankets and rope. Chrysion rode the horse until Contus grew tired, then they switched.

After the ten-mile journey into town, they realized they were overdue for a bath. The inn they chose had no bathing facility. The innkeeper advised they go to the thermae, a traditional bath. When they arrived, the attendant showed them to the changing room. After removing their vestments, a boy took their belongings and placed them in a locked chest, giving the key to Chrysion. The boy stole nervous glances at Contus's magnificent appendage, but he said nothing.

In the thermopolis, or steam bath, the elephantine cock raised eyebrows and evoked whispers from the men sitting in a circle around the steaming stones.

Contus spied one man whose smile made the room lighter. They sat beside him. On closer inspection, they could see a caste in one eye rendering him partially blind.

The man extended a hand. "Kolossos." Neither Chrysion nor Contus knew much of the Macedonian tongue, but they were able to introduce themselves. Unlike the others in the room, Kolossos wore a towel. He repeated his name, then pointed to his crotch. He opened the towel, revealing a massive cock. A colossus, of course!

Chrysion asked in broken Macedonian, "Do you speak Thracian?"

"Thracian? I am from Thrace! Of course, I do!"

It was a relief to meet a countryman. He touched his giant cock and said, "Do you want to play?" He put a hand under Chrysion's buttocks and wiggled a finger into the loose hole.

Chrysion was startled by the man's boldness. Contus laughed and said, "I believe we have met the first church member."

The three men left the steam room, Contus grabbing a wooden rinsing bowl from the shower room. They went to the toilets, the darkest room in the bath, and Kolossos locked the door.

"We must stop if someone requires the toilet, but it's rare." They were in near darkness, for this room's only light source was candlelight from the hallway. With the door shut, the air was the color of squid ink.

Kolossos sat on a toilet seat, his enormous penis towering skyward. Chrysion sat on it, surprised by how thick it was. He wondered if he could take Contus at the same time. He chuckled. Of course, he could. He had devoted his ass to cock, and it would not suddenly lose its faith.

When Chrysion was settled in Kolossos's lap, Contus lifted his lover's legs towards the ceiling, exposing the hole he knew so well. It was tight, perhaps too tight. With great force, he pushed the swollen apple into his lover. Kolossos was deep in the second chamber. The passageway was cramped, but Contus found entry to the third chamber with great effort. He heard his lover cry out.

"Are you okay?"

Chrysion shook his head, but Contus couldn't see in the dark.

He repeated.

Chrysion spoke. "It hurts terribly, but I will heal."

"May I continue?"

"Yes. I need communion."

Contus became trapped in the third chamber. He could move back and forth, but the corona of his cock was like an arrowhead; it could not move in reverse past the huge thick cock of their fellow countryman. So Contus moved in small, rapid strokes.

"Oh! Oh! That is incredible!" Kolossos shivered with ecstasy. When Chrysion spasmed, he cried out. It was agony and pleasure in equal measure. There was no give; it was like a tree lodged in his entrails. When his innards contracted, they hurt.

Contus heard the signal. Chrysion panted like a dog on a hot day. Contus was so familiar with his lover that he caught his semen even in the pitch dark. He held the sweet liquid in front of Kolossos, who sipped it.

"Oh, that's sweet! Oh! Why does it tingle so?"

Contus said, "It's holy communion. First the boy, then the man."

"Whatever it is, I will soon lose my seed inside the boy."

Chrysion spoke between moans. "It won't be lost."

The boy's moans became pants, then a loud cry. Contus caught his lover's second flow, feeding it to their friend and Chrysion before lapping up the remains.

"Oh, for the love of cock! I'm going to blast inside you!" Kolossos was wedged so tightly there was no room for his seed to spill. It stretched the second chamber before finally bursting into the third.

Contus was able to move smoothly after that blast. Chrysion's entrails were slick with sperm, and Kolossos's tumescence had subsided slightly. Contus finished at the deepest point in his lover's gut, at the seventh rib.

A knock came at the door.

"One minute!" Kolossos tried to withdraw and couldn't. Contus had him pinned to the walls of Chrysion's chambers.

Contus grabbed the bowl and placed it beneath Chrysion's anus. Together, the two men pulled out. Kolossos's seed spilled out with his cock, and Contus's semen was quick to follow. The bowl filled with the endless load and threatened to overflow.

Another insistent knock. "It's urgent! Please hurry!"

Kolossos unlocked the door, letting in the light. The frustrated patron sat on a toilet and loudly shat. Contus rushed to Chrysion's side. His lover was doubled over, semen running from his ass.

The communion bowl overflowed with the divine host. Chrysion couldn't wait; he needed the healing power immediately. He skipped turns and drank a large helping from the bowl. He sighed. A thin trickle of blood ran down his leg.

Contus grabbed his lover by the arm. "Are you injured?"

"Nothing that communion won't heal."

Kolossos saw the bowl. "What is that for?"

"Communion. Healing. If you drink that, your eye will heal."

Kolossos frowned. "Blindness can't be healed."

Contus passed him the bowl. "Trust me."

Kolossos sipped the communion seed. "It is good!" He drank again. They passed the bowl until they were very full. Like drunkenness, but with visions, they became intoxicated on the solid brew. In the steam room, the tendrils of water licked the ceiling and formed ghostly shapes. Kolossos began to laugh and could not stop. "I feel as though I have smoked Asterion!"

For an hour, the men remained inebriated. They soaked in the hot bath water, jumped into the icy water, then soaked in tepid water. Kolossos and Contus drew much attention with their enormous genitals, while Chrysion attracted a different breed of man with his perfectly round butt and tiny penis. All who approached heard tell of the church forming in Thessaloniki. Kolossos would be the leader with his mighty cock and massive estate overlooking the harbor. The first meeting would be on the morrow at sundown.

CHAPTER 3

Kolossos insisted the two lovers stay with him. He had servants retrieve their horse and belongings from the inn while his cook prepared a seafood feast. After a fish and shrimp soup, smoked octopus, fried squid, sturgeon eggs, and roast sea bass landed on the table in courses. They drank heavily of the wine imported from Latium outside Rome. The meal was so delicious, Chrysion nearly wept, and he dabbed at his eyes with a linen napkin. When the meal had settled, the last course arrived: a delicate pastry made of hundreds of thin sheets of dough stuffed with honey, rose water, and walnuts.

Bellies distended, the men retired to their chambers and fell asleep.

In the morning, Kolossos gave the two lovers a tour of the estate. The villa consisted of a dozen large rooms surrounding a central courtyard. On the grounds were a large barn for horses, a ball court, a cooling shed, and a modest temple dedicated to Hermes. The temple was in the middle of an olive orchard.

Kolossos said, "These trees have many buds, but the

fruit will not be ready until the spring produces fruit and the summer sun ripens it. It is autumn, and the harvest is over."

Wide, cushioned benches lined the temple walls. A large stone table sat at the center. In the middle of the table was a marble statue of Hermes, with a proudly erect penis.

Kolossos said, "Hermes's temple will be perfect for this evening's worship."

And it was.

When evening came, dozens of men appeared for worship. Inside the temple, foods befitting an orgy adorned the central table. Inside the entrance stood the three men naked. First Kolossos, then Contus, then Chrysion. As the first man entered the temple, he knelt and kissed the two massive cocks, then Chrysion's beautiful behind. He touched a finger to his lips and then his forehead. The sight of this made all three men very hard. The next man had no need to kneel. He bent slightly to kiss Kolossos, stood straight to kiss Contus, then stooped to kiss the perfect behind of Chrysion. A tradition was born in those moments that may last for eons. The simple kiss of devotion upon entering the temple was simple, practical, and beautiful.

By the time the sun touched the horizon, each man had received twice a dozen kisses. The temple had nearly reached capacity on its very first day!

Contus addressed the assembly. "My cock is the source of the great seed, and the great seed is but one portion of the blessed communion. Chrysion's small, sweet seed is the fruit of the union and must be consumed for communion to be complete. Kolossos, your host, has been given holy communion, so his cock is now a permanent source of the great seed. We will find among you a novitiate with little length or girth; they will be your permanent source of sweet seed. Who offers their backside to Kolossos?

A young man, slender with brown hair and green eyes, stepped forward. "I am Teodoros, and I shall commune."

While men of all shapes and sizes stroked their cocks, Kolossos licked Teodoros's hole. Next, he stood, his cock at full mast, and pushed the head inside. The handsome novitiate cried out in agony. When his cries reduced to whimpers, Kolossos went further inside.

"Your hole resists my mighty cock. Shall I stop?"

Teodoros shook his head. "I am learning to accommodate you. Please continue."

While Kolossos trained his novitiate, Contus entered the blissful doorway between Chrysion's buttocks. He felt good to be with his beloved before a crowd. Chrysion moaned with pleasure. His hole was a wide hallway now and gave little resistance to the obscenely large cock of the demigod.

Kolossos buried himself to the hilt. Teodoros opened his mouth in a silent cry of joy. One by one, men stepped forward and fed their modest cocks to him and Chrysion. They erupted quickly, for such was the sexual energy in the temple that it echoed off the walls. Chrysion and Teodoros hungrily swallowed the seed and opened their mouths again for the next in line. In total, twenty members gave their sacred nectar to the two young men.

When all were sated, Contus and Kolossos filled the colons of the two novitiates. A member grasped an enormous fruit bowl from the center table, emptying it. The leader and the demigod then filled the vessel with the holy seed. Kolossos marveled at the volume of semen he had produced. It was tenfold the usual amount. But even with the demigod's bushel of sperm, the bowl was half-filled.

Kolossos clapped his hands. "We need each of you to spill communion seed in one of the catamites."

The men who fed the semen to the boys were required to produce more. Though they were of all ages and sizes, the reverberation of sexual power gave them a second wind. A gray-haired man stepped forward and entered Teodoros with ease. A man with jet black hair and a hairy chest produced an enormous erection and put it inside Chrysion. Kolossos added his cock beside that of the gray-haired man, and Contus joined the dark-haired man inside Chrysion. Each man whose cock came in contact with that of Kolossos or Contus became aware of a tingling sensation as the power of communion passed from cock to cock. Small bolts of lightning traveled up their spines when they came, making their heads grow heavy. They retired to a bench to recover.

The remaining men formed two lines - large cocks for Chrysion, average to small for Teodoros. The transfer of cock energy continued for several hours until every man was satisfied. Chrysion squatted over the bowl and emptied his bowels of the fruit of ten men's cocks. Teodoros did the same. Then at midnight, the bowl was passed from mouth to mouth as the First Phallic Church of Thessaloniki inaugurated its new temple with sacred communion.

Contus spoke: "Go forth, initiates, for as long as one High Priest and one Leader are present, you may pass the power to others. May the Phallic Brotherhood multiply in numbers."

But the festivities had only just begun. The semen's power granted sacred visions of ghostly apparitions, colored lights, and dragon's teeth. The men cleared the central table, and all willing catamites lay on their backs with their holes exposed. Men filled those holes with earthly flesh and Olympian semen. The orgy continued until the sun's first rays scraped the dawn sky. They produced much semen, not all of it making its way into bowls, for the orgy had spilled out of the temple into the olive orchard. Every last man had satisfied their primal lust.

CHAPTER 4

Kolossos, Contus, and Chrysion collapsed into a large bed to sleep off the night's excesses. They awoke that afternoon when a servant rushed into the room.

"Kolossos, sir, you must come see."

The two lovers and the wealthy merchant followed the servant to the orchard. To their astonishment, the trees bore bright green olives.

Kolossos was dumbstruck. "This miracle shall make me a wealthier man indeed!"

The seed spilled the previous night had passed its fertility and power into the orchard. From that day forward, all olive trees bore fruit in September and ripened by January.

"Surely I will share this knowledge with the worshippers so that they may spill their sacred seed in their own gardens."

Contus said, "It must be the seed of a catamite, spilled by pleasure alone, with no masturbation."

Kolossos stared at the phallic god. The cloud had disappeared from his eye. "How do you know this?"

Contus shrugged. "I don't know how; I just do."

The temple of Phallic Worship at Uskudama took seven seasons to establish, but here in Thessaloniki, it was already twenty members strong. In Thrace, the men were less interested in fucking boys, and their society looked down on the practice. Macedonia had a reputation for more liberal sexual freedom; men and boys lay with each other as a matter of course. Macedonian soldiers kept male lovers. Thus the church was ripe for establishment. Add to that the prosperity and fertility produced by the communion, and a cult was sure to form.

Over the next month, Kolossos hosted Saturday night orgies in the temple of Hermes. The semen from the catamites, produced without manual stimulation, was consumed for strength, health, and wealth. The remainder was so powerful that a single drop of communion semen spilled in a garden would yield a bountiful harvest. The legend of Contus Pedalis grew with each orgy. Hundreds of worshippers packed the temple until there was no room. Kolossos had a makeshift annex built to house the swelling crowd.

The worshippers had no book to guide them, so their stories of the power of Contus and Chrysion were whispered from ear to ear, growing wilder and more fantastic with each telling.

Chrysion overheard a novitiate saying, "Contus was born from the very cock of Zeus himself. His powers come from Mount Olympus."

A man with a long thin cock said, "I can thicken my pole by merely entering the ass of Chrysion."

A poet, short in stature and hung very small, said, "I want Contus inside me. He will make my headaches go away."

The poet's friend responded, "Any man with sufficient cock now carries the power of Contus. Lay with the first man you see."

The three founders of the church gathered in the main hall on a Sunday afternoon to discuss the chaotic growth of the cult of Contus Pedalis.

Contus said, "My guardians gave me a Roman name, but for the cult to thrive, it must be in a language that will last, such as the Athenian tongue."

It was true that Latin had produced few scholarly works, and Greek was the language of philosophers, poets, and mathematicians. Kolossos nodded his assent.

Chrysion said, "We can't just call it the Church of Cock; it will offend women and priests."

Kolossos agreed. "Pedalis means twelve inches, yet

you are so much larger than your name. Let us then call your cock by its measure. *Paykos* is a cubit, the measure of a man's arm from fingertip to elbow."

Contus said, "The temple of the cubit lacks something."

Chrysion said, "The cubit is sacred. *Hagia*."

Contus shook his head. "Hagiapaykus" is ugly.

Kolossos smiled. "What about *pria*? Beloved?"

Chrysion clapped his hands. "The Temple of Priapaykos!"

Kolossos shook his head. "In truth, I would say two cubits is more accurate, but *priabipaykos* is unpleasant to the ear, so why don't we instead just say a foot, just like your own last name? *Priapous* the beloved twelve inches."

Contus grinned. "I like it. No, I love it."

The next order of business was to write a holy book to outline the rules and beliefs of the worshippers.

"I volunteer, for I know how to write," said Chrysion. "I will begin with the fundamental rules of worship, but then I will also tell the story of Contus Pedalis and his sacred semen."

The three agreed that Chrysion should write the rules and the gospel of Priapous. The first high priest of the Temple of Priapous committed the rites to scrolls.

CHAPTER 5 - TEMPLE BYLAWS

The Temple is a community committed to recognizing the divinity of the phallus in all its forms. So, too, is the semen, the sacred covenant of communion between man and Priapous. Here are the sacred tenets:

1. Anywhere two or more men gather is the temple.

2. So long as one of the men has taken communion from another member of the temple, the union is sacred.
3. To worship, the man with the largest phallus must insert it into the hole of the smallest man.
4. Communion consists of three sexual acts: the insertion of the large phallus, the spontaneous ejaculation of the small phallus, and the spilling of the seed of the large phallus in the chambers of the smallest man.
5. Communion continues with the consumption of the seed. First, catch the semen of the smaller member in the palm of a large hand and drink thereof. Second, catch the seed of the large phallus by spilling it into a bowl, then drink therefrom.
6. The act of communion in large gatherings shall see the next largest member commune with the next smallest member.
7. Communion may be taken directly from the source via the act of oral worship.
8. Two large men may penetrate the smaller man when desired, thereby doubling the bounty.
9. Spilling seed is not forbidden but is wasteful.
10. For a smaller man to manually stimulate himself is allowed but is less sacred than spontaneous ejaculation.
11. At any gathering, the member of the temple with the largest phallus is the Leader, and the man with the smallest is the high priest.
12. A man shall be deemed small and engage as a catamite (passive) when his erection is not long enough for the entire head to pass the second ring of the anus.

13. A man shall be deemed large and engage as a pedicant (active) if the corona passes the second ring and fully enters the rectum.
14. A man shall be deemed sacred either if his cock be long enough to enter the second chamber or so short that he cannot use it for insertive sex.
15. Group worship shall take place Saturday nights in a location selected for its seclusion and capacity to hold a gathering.
16. Members of Temple Priapous may seek communion with other members at any time. See Tenet I
17. Because communion is sacred and open to all, members should avoid refusing communion with another member.
18. If one member refuses communion to another, the second man shall not force communion or retaliate against the first.
19. Members are comrades of the phallic brotherhood. As such, they shall treat one another with dignity and respect.
20. The erect phallus is a manifestation of the gods and a sign of their wisdom, grace, and generosity.

Kolossos hired a mason to carve the twenty tenets into a marble tablet, which he then placed on the temple's rear wall for all to read.

CHAPTER 6

Seasons passed. Saturday nights at the temple were always crowded to capacity with naked men, fucking and sucking to their hearts' content. The seed was gathered and distributed. Feeding it to one's bulls made many cows give birth. Sprinkling it in a vegetable patch would ensure a rich harvest. Men grew wealthy by soaking a coin in the semen. The bounty that Priapous promised was so attractive even the most pious man would set aside his beliefs for a night of debauchery and pleasure, knowing they would receive more than they gave.

One Saturday night, exhausted from the excesses of pleasure, Contus sat in the orchard upon a stone bench and rested. His serpentine cock hung from his groin, resting on the fertile soil. Chrysion, drunk on semen, sat on his lap, stroking the massive member. It rose from the ground and stretched skyward. Chrysion discovered he was ensnared in a cock trap that held him pinned to his beloved.

From a nearby olive branch came a familiar trill; it was the dove.

She sang:

> *In Saloniki, you have built*
> *A temple to the phallus*
> *That fills its faithful to the hilt*
> *And brings luck to the palace.*
>
> *But time moves on you must depart*
> *For elsewhere you shall nourish.*
> *Across the sea is Hellespont*
> *Where Priapous will flourish.*

And away flew the dove once again.

Kolossos learned of the message and grew despondent. He felt genuine love for both men, erotic, friendly, and familiar. To lose such friends would tie like cords around his heart. But he understood the campaign to establish the Temple of Priapous did not end in Thessaloniki.

Lying unclothed in his bed with the two lovers, he said, "My dear friends, how can I bid thee adieu? My heart pains me to think of my bed empty once more."

Contus wiped away a tear. "As we once filled your bed, so too shall another."

Kolossos sighed. "I have fucked a thousand catamites but have only ever loved one." He looked at Chrysion and winked.

Chrysion smiled. "Teodoros has confided to me that he would gladly take my place by your side."

Teodoros, the first novitiate, was the first man Kolossos fucked after receiving his communion. He had a shapely bottom and a perfect tiny penis, one-tenth the size of Kolossos.

"Next Saturday, I shall seek him out and beat his innards with my club," said Kolossos.

Chrysion said, "Don't forget the gentle kisses and manly caresses. His bottom will thank you for showing mercy."

The men laughed.

Kolossos stood, his heavy member swinging between his legs. "I command a fleet of merchant ships. One shall take you to Hellespont to the port of Lampsacus, and I'll remain behind to spread the good news westward. From Lampsacus, you can reach all of Asia Minor and the Levant."

"I have a parting gift for you," said Chrysion. "I have communed directly with so many men that I have learned to open my mouth beyond limits. I wish to take communion from your loins as no one else has ever done."

Kolossos showed tumescence; his member grew and began its journey skyward. "You would do that for me?"

The boy nodded. "Nothing would make me happier." He knelt on the bed, his mouth at waist level. The fearsome cock, with its angry red head, hovered midair. Chrysion held the colossus with both hands to steady it. He clamped his mouth over the opening and unhinged his jaw. With ease, he took the fist-sized head into his mouth. Kolossos exhaled loudly.

Contus watched the communion unfolding, and he felt the familiar swelling between his legs. The enormous cock stretched and yawned as it lifted off the bed. Contus moved closer to his lover, so the hard head rested on Chrysion's backside.

"May I?"

Chrysion answered with mouth full. "Mmm."

Contus made his cock slick with olive oil, then pressed against the hole of the boy he loved, the only one who could ever take him. With slight pressure, he pushed past the gates into the first chamber. He rose to one knee to move into the second chamber. He walked forward on both knees, holding Chrysion by the waist to keep him steady. He reached the third chamber as his pubic mound came to rest on the ample buttocks.

Chrysion was taking communion at both ends. It excited him so much that he shuddered, achieving orgasm effortlessly. Contus put a big hand under the boy's tiny penis and caught the flow. He fed it to Kolossos, then the boy, and took the last bit himself.

Kolossos shed tears of joy. "I never thought I would know this feeling. How grateful I am to have it once in this life!"

The demigod felt the familiar churn of Chrysion's innards. It felt like a thousand tiny hands were stroking his cock from stem to stern. "By the gods, Chrysion, you were delivered to me. I thank each of them. Oh!" The waves of contraction grew more intense so that the thousand hands joined together to become five hundred, then two hundred fifty, then fifty, then 25, then 10, and at last, the waves came together in a single intense stroke that ran the entire length of Contus's mighty cock.

"I cannot last long!"

Kolossos got another huge surprise. Chrysion grabbed him by the buttocks and pulled him to him, letting the huge cock slide down his throat. He bobbed up and down, holding his breath, keeping the monster lodged in his throat, but stroking it with his gullet.

"By all the gods, Chrysion, never have I felt such pleasure!" Kolossos began fucking the boy's throat. He withdrew enough to give him breath, then plunged back down. "It's better than any cunt or ass. Ohhh!"

Contus, meanwhile, was at the precipice. "I cannot hold it any longer. Uhhh!" With that, he flooded Chrysion's bowels with his manly fluid.

Kolossos could hear the raging river flow from Contus, which put him over the edge. "Oh, gods! I'm coming!" Chrysion pulled him close, so the endless flow of semen bypassed the boy's mouth and flowed straight to his stomach.

As always, Chrysion became so ecstatic from sex that his penis spat out another helping of high priest communion, which they shared all around.

Kolossos softened, but Chrysion clung to the enormous cock, nursing its final drops. At last, he let the beast go, and it smacked Kolossos loudly on the lower thigh.

The wash basin caught the huge ejaculation as it flowed from Chrysion's bum. All three men drank to their fill, but much was still left. Rather than see it go to waste, they went to the citrus grove and scattered it among the lemon trees. Blossoms appeared instantly.

GOSPEL OF PRIAPUS BOOK THREE

Being the account of a perilous journey, the march to Lampsacus, the conversion of the Centurions, and the elevation of Priapus and Chrysion to immortal gods in the wood and fruit of the fig tree.

CHAPTER 1

The next morning, the two lovers gathered their belongings and followed Kolossos to the port. There they saw great vessels unloading spices from the Indus and bolts of fabric from silken Samarkand. Kolossos navigated the busy harbor with the confidence befitting a powerful merchant.

A sun-baked man called out, "Ho! Kolossos! 'Tis I, Damian!"

He approached with a broad smile, one hand outstretched.

They shook hands, demonstrating that they were equals under Hellenic democracy. Damian wore a tunic that had only one sleeve. His right nipple was exposed, and he wore a ring in it, which excited Chrysion greatly. His excitement did not go unnoticed by the handsome captain. He patted the boy on his rump and said, "May ye open to my bidding, lad." It was friendly chatter, but it bore a menace beneath the smile.

Kolossos grew melancholy. "Here is where I bid ye farewell, dear comrades." He opened his powerful arms wide and welcomed both men in his wide embrace. He kissed Chrysion's hair and Contus's lips. "Damian will care for your every need, and I have paid him well."

Damian gave a mischievous smile. "Aye, that you did, Kolossos." He put an arm around the two men. "My most precious cargo."

Kolossos wiped a tear and waved farewell.

Contus was far too innocent to detect what Chrysion had. Damian was without conscience. He was untrustworthy. But Kolossos had chosen him out of his whole fleet, so he must be good at his job. Or so they believed.

Damian steered the two lovers away from their dear friend towards his ship. "Here she is. This is Niki."

He pointed to the impressive vessel with 90 oar holes per side.

Chrysion marveled at the size. "It's so big!"

Damian grabbed his crotch and waggled his cock under the tunic. "That's what the ladies say. And the boy-whores too." He frowned when neither laughed at his joke. "The hold is filled with Amphorae of Olive Oil, Wool, and Oregano. Bound for Rodos."

Chrysion frowned. "Rodos? That is not on the way to Lampsacus."

Damian snarled. "Kolossos paid me well but not well enough to give up my trade. We will gather cargo in Rodos bound for Lampsacus."

Contus opened his mouth to speak, but Chrysion squeezed his hand and shook his head softly. The ensuing silence gave discomfort to all three.

The ship raised its sails and pulled away from the port. Chrysion had the urge to jump overboard, but he knew it was too late. To confirm his fears, he said, "Where do we sleep?"

"With the other slaves!"

Contus said, "Slaves? Whatever do you mean?"

"I mean, you're locked in the hold, and you won't see full daylight until I'm finished with the both of you."

He pushed Contus down the stairs. Chrysion ran after, but Damian grabbed him by the neck. "Not yet. I have more for you!"

He picked up the small youth and carried him to his cabin, throwing him roughly on the bed. "You know what comes next."

"Face or Buttocks?" Chrysion's former life as a paid catamite would serve him well in these moments."

"Let me see that beautiful behind." The sailor roughly grabbed the tunic and lifted it. He spread the cheeks and tasted the hole.

"Have you been lying with horses? Why is this so loose?"

Chrysion realized at that moment that his lover's big secret had escaped Damian's eye. A man like Damian thought only of his own cock and had no cause to notice another.

"I was a catamite in Istambolia. The men there are rather large."

When Damian pulled out his hard cock, it was a relief. It was short and narrow. "Perhaps the mouth will be tighter." And indeed, he meant mouth, for his penis could not reach the throat.

The sailor grabbed Chrysion by the ears and shoved his cock into the pretty mouth. Chrysion knew well the trick to make any man feel bigger. He tightened his lips and pretended to gag.

"Do you enjoy my cock in your mouth?"

Chrysion nodded. It was mostly a lie. He tasted salt on his tongue, a signal that this seafaring rogue was near orgasm. Reaching up a hand, Chrysion tugged on the nipple ring.

"Oh, gods, that feels great!" Damian threw his head back and roared.

A small helping of sperm filled Chrysion's mouth. Damian watched him closely. "You'd best not spit that out, boy. Swallow it."

It had been many moons since Chrysion had tasted unconsecrated sperm, and it was bitter. He forced the milky brew down his throat, gagging for real this time.

Damian had no pretense of passion, love, or care. He escorted Chrysion to the hatch and pushed him. Chrysion nearly lost footing as he went into the inky gloom.

"I expect you'll provide me service again. Be prepared."

CHAPTER 2

As Chrysion's eyes adjusted to the darkness, he spat to remove the acrid taste from his mouth.

"Chrysion?" He heard his lover calling from a nearby bunk. He followed the voice to Contus.

"What did he do to you?"

Chrysion shrugged. "Nothing that hasn't been done to me many times."

"We have to share a bunk, and it's cramped." Contus showed him the hard wood that formed their bread. Chrysion took the pack with their belongings and re-moved a large wool blanket.

Contus hopped down, and the two folded the blanket to fit the space. It was much softer. They made a pillow of their winter tunic made of soft, thick cotton yarn.

"It's still very tight. Can we both fit?"

Chrysion smiled. "We'll gain much space if you fuck me to sleep and leave it in."

Such language excited Contus; his member began to swell. Chrysion lay atop it.

"Sorry, but we must keep this a secret. Damian is a loose hinge, and he will take your size as a great insult."

"With your body so close to mine, I fear it won't go down."

There were nearly two hundred slaves that shared the quarters with them. Many spoke strange tongues from the Levant, Egypt, or Libya; others were from Dacia, Gallia, and other far-flung provinces of the Roman Empire. But one slave, old and infirm, spoke the tongue of Anatolya.

"Friends, fortune has brought you to me. For three long years, I have been unable to speak my mother tongue, and to hear it from your lips is music indeed."

Chrysion extended a hand and introduced himself and his lover.

The old man said, "I am Ibrahim. I'm grateful for your presence."

"And I you," said Chrysion.

Ibrahim beamed. "Such a beautiful visage you have. So, too, does your friend Contus."

Contus smiled. "Thank you. I rarely get compliments on my face."

Chrysion squeezed his hand to remind him of the secret.

Ibrahim leaned in close. "I overheard you. Please know that your big secret is safe with me. And you're right to believe that Damian would be jealous. But I am curious to see it all the same."

Chrysion said, "When it is safe to do so, you will see it."

Ibrahim gave the lovers a tour of the floating prison named Niki. The living quarters were in the center of the ship, while the outer portion consisted of rows of benches and long oars.

"We are in high winds now, but between here and

Rodos, there may be doldrums. We will break our backs in those still waters.

At the ship's rear were toilets arranged in a semicircle with no door. Several men were shitting in plain sight, speaking a strange tongue.

One of the men shouted at Ibrahim, and Ibrahim called back in the strange tongue and laughed.

"Those men are Trojans. Soldiers who lost their freedom in wars with Sparta and Athens."

Contus looked at their new friend. "What did they say to you?"

Ibrahim laughed. "They told me to paint a portrait of them sitting upon the commode so I won't stare any longer, and I returned the insult by saying it was only worthy of a love poem."

Chrysion asked, "How many languages do you speak?"

Ibrahim rubbed his chin. I don't know the count, but I speak six well enough to jest. There are maybe twenty others I know enough to get by.

Ibrahim next led them to the dining area at the front of the ship.

"We are treated as horses. They give us only enough fuel to row: bread, olive oil, and sheep cheese. They feed us sausage at the solstice and the equinox but no wine. I have gone far too long without wine."

Contus smiled. "I can produce a drink more intoxicating than wine and more fortifying than sausage."

Chrysion spoke. "Ibrahim, I have been jailed once. In jail, every man finds a mate. Have our fellow slaves found love in this manner?"

Ibrahim nodded. "We come from many places. Most believe that there is shame in being a bottom or catamite. So we have very few couples. Ten very busy young men accommodate the needs of the rest."

Chrysion put together pieces of a puzzle. "Are there men who wish to stay here on the ship?"

Ibrahim shook his head. "No one wishes to stay."

"Are any loyal to Damian or his crew?"

Ibrahim thought hard. "There are three young catamites who serve his needs, and he grants them special favors. Are you planning something?"

Chrysion shrugged. "Contus and I are in service to man. We raise the spirit through communion. It is powerful medicine."

"Communion? Eat in union...what is that?"

"We eat together. The body and the blood of the demigod in our midst. But before doing such things, we must know it will remain a secret from the captain and crew."

Ibrahim hopped from one foot to another. "I will make it my task to swear every last slave to secrecy. If one refuses, we will tie him to the center mast."

A bell rang. "It's time for our meal. Come."

CHAPTER 3

The three sat at a long table surrounded by many men of all shapes, sizes, colors, and countries. At their table were the Persians and Egyptians at opposite ends, and Dacians sat in the middle. Ibrahim engaged each group in their own language, letting them know of the great miracle among them and swearing them to secrecy. The three groups complied. Ibrahim left their table and went to a small table where only young men dined. These catamites all spoke a blended tongue of Athenian and Roman. Ibrahim gestured carefully and studied the faces of the young men. He spent more time with three whom Chrysion assumed were favorites of Damian. They looked somewhat like him; all were fair-haired and small in stature.

Ibrahim returned to the table. "I think we can trust all but one catamite. Not Iulian, the Dacian. He is loyal only to Damian."

Chrysion said, "Does he know what we are planning?"

Ibrahim shook his head. "I had to test first to see where loyalties lay. I made no mention of the secret to any of them."

Meal time came to an end. There were approximately twenty men who would cooperate, nine who seemed likely, and one who would cause problems, Iulian of Dacia.

Contus watched his lover and Ibrahim strategize. He was too pure to understand how men require manipulation to comply. His knowledge of politics was almost nil.

The few rays of sunlight that lit the slaves' quarters vanished. The moonlight was a poor light source, and there were no candles or lanterns. It was time for rest.

Contus climbed into the bunk first. It was so dark nobody could see what they did next. Chrysion rubbed the head of Contus's cock until it rose to his chest. Chrysion sat on Contus's shoulder and took the massive cock inside him. He had to change positions as the cock turned corners, but at long last, it was wedged solidly inside him, near the ribs. Chrysion turned his head and planted his lips on Contus's. In rhythmic waves, Chrysion moved his bottom, using his insides to stroke his lover's enormous cock.

"Oh, that feels good, Chrysion."

Chrysion said, "It does."

In this way, the fair-haired youth brought his lover toward orgasm in slow, gentle strokes. As free men, they were rough and quick with their sexual union. But here, in the blackness of night, surrounded by two hundred slaves, they were forced to move slowly. Chrysion held his hand to his belly, where he felt the giant log of flesh moving inside him. Contus felt the pressure, and it excited him. He increased the speed of his strokes, stretching the third chamber as more blood filled his member. The waves of muscle contractions began, bringing both men closer to orgasm.

Chrysion panted. "I'm there." Contus caught the sweet semen in his hand, fed it to his lover, and then ate the rest. Chrysion's taste and fragrance were a direct link to Aphrodite. Contus's cock swelled and stretched, filling the youth completely while wave after wave rocked his slender body until he ejaculated again. The second dose of semen was the tipping point for Contus, who could no longer retain his seed. The slow sex had caused him to stretch so deep and wide that his semen couldn't stay in the third chamber and flowed into the fourth.

Chrysion spoke. "We'll have to wait until morning to release the communion from my bowels."

Bound together by the huge cock, the lovers drifted into sleep.

CHAPTER 4

The following day, Chrysion retrieved a wash basin from their bag. He had packed it for the journey, not knowing if such things existed on ships. Perhaps they did, but not in the slave quarters. In the tight space, it was hard for the two lovers to separate and catch the flow in the basin, but they managed. The basin only filled halfway, as Chrysion's body had absorbed much of the communion. What came out was thicker than usual, like porridge, and very easy to eat with their fingers. As slaves passed by on their way to the toilets, they spied the strange couple eating porridge from a giant bowl. Contus grew a thick beard after eating the concentrated semen.

There were no bathing facilities in the slaves' quarters, but enough sea water entered through small holes, filling buckets. Men were able to wash themselves with their hands. Contus was afraid to show himself, but

Ibrahim reassured him. Iulian always sees Damian in the cuddy after he showers. There he is now.

Ibrahim nodded in the direction of a young man with long brown hair, no beard or body hair, and a plump bottom.

Iulian dressed and whistled for one of the crew to escort him above deck. When he was gone, Ibrahim jumped on a table and shouted in vulgar Latin, which could be understood or translated by many slaves.

"Fellow slaves! We have among us a god. Before the helmsman and his musicians arrive, let me tell you of our impending freedom! None of us should remain in bondage, but we are weak and malnourished. They don't give us the beans that any ship would give. Are you hungry?"

The oarsmen looked from one to the other in puzzlement.

Ibrahim repeated, "I can't hear you! Are you hungry?"

"Yes!" a handful of oarsmen shouted.

"No one else? Are you hungry?"

Now the cabin filled with a resounding shout. "Yes!"

"Well, gentlemen, I have food for your body and soul. When you partake in it, you will grow stronger. And as a unit, we can overthrow this illegal slaver and his wretched ship!"

A Phoenician slave shouted, "What is this food you speak of?"

Ibrahim smiled. "I'm glad you asked, sir. It's the nectar of the gods, or of one god, to be precise. And you will see its source, for he lives among us and has come to save us all."

Contus disrobed and showered himself with the cold seawater. The men crowded around, gasping and pointing in amazement.

"Surely he is a god, the son of Zarathustra himself!" said one Babylonian.

"Nay, he is Zeus's offspring!" a Macedonian argued.

The oarsmen quibbled amongst themselves. Ibrahim stood tall. "He is a god unlike any other. He belongs to no other god, nor is he a single god of the Israelites. Worship him, and your crops will grow. Commune of his seed and your bodies will strengthen. Welcome him into your hearts, and you will have freedom."

The ship's hatch opened, and Paleos, the helmsman, descended with his piper and singer. Contus threw on his tunic, covering his magic pole.

"The winds are unfavorable. We will row to Rodos."

Paleos saw the men gathered in a vast circle around one man. "What is this?"

Ibrahim hopped down from the table. "We were certain there would be rowing today, so we chanted to raise our energy levels. Having no beans to fuel our bodies, we are sorely in need of courage."

The helmsman nodded. "You show good initiative, men. I agree; you should be fed and given rest. Not only because it makes my work all the more difficult but also for the shame it brings this ship to treat men so. Slavery is not a democratic institution."

Ibrahim translated for the men.

An Egyptian asked, "Is he with us?"

Ibrahim held a finger to his lips.

The piper and singer stood at the helm. The aulos flute played a lively tune, and the singer started to chant in a dialect no one understood, but all obeyed. For as his song gathered speed, the oars moved faster, too. The work was painful and exhausting. There were 170 oars and 200 men. They moved in and out in shifts of 30.

When Chrysion and Contus received respite, they nearly collapsed. They leaned on each other for support, then moved to the back of the ship and lay on their bunks. There was neither water nor food. Nor was there any place where they could take communion to rebuild their strength. No sooner had they regained their breath when they were called back to the oars for many more hours of grueling labor. The rowing continued for several days. Nobody was permitted to sleep for more than a few minutes. In this way, they could not celebrate communion on the open sea.

CHAPTER 5

Rodos is a distant island, far south and far east of Thessaloniki. They could be there in four days with favorable winds assisting the oars. On the fourth day, the ship passed under the Colossus and into the harbor at Rhodes.

The slaves remained below decks, locked in their quarters. Ibrahim gathered the slaves and began the complex process of organizing men for communion. The ten catamites were to serve 190 men, which would take too long. So, more men volunteered as hosts to receive communion in their holes, whether mouth or anus.

The ceremony began with Contus and Chrysion. One by one, the most well-endowed members of the rowing crew, many quite impressive, joined their cocks with Contus inside Chrysion, then drank the sweet nectar from the boy's tiny penis and the meal that spilled from his ass. These men were then free to go to the next catamite, with whom one would pedicate, and the other would irrumate, and in this way, communion spread from man to man. The entire crew, including fair-haired Iulian of Dacia, were in this way initiated into the cult of Priapous. Immediately, the men felt their muscles grow more substantial and their cocks grow harder. The ceremony concluded with passing the bowl of Contus's semen that had spilled from Chrysion's backside. From one man to the next, each took but a small sip, which was enough to send a jolt of god-like energy through their weary bodies.

With the power of the Priapic god at their heels, the men stormed the hold, forcing the iron bars out of their wooden frames. Two hundred angry men spilled onto the top deck. The ship was in the harbor, and the free sailors were away on shore leave. Only Paleos, the helmsman, the chanter, and the piper were left to watch the ship.

Upon seeing an angry mob break through the hold, he sat in prayer, holding his knees to his chest. The men were not angry with him. Ibrahim put a reassuring hand on his shoulder. "Brother, it is your choice; take communion with us and join us or disembark. We are setting sail for freedom."

Paleos stood, unsure of what was meant by the choice Ibrahim gave. "You are leaving? How is it that you broke through the iron bars?"

Ibrahim explained communion. Paleos shook his head in disbelief. "If I hadn't just witnessed you destroy your prison gates, I would doubt you. But surely a miracle is taking place."

At that moment, Contus approached. "Salve, Paleos."

The helmsman saw the outline of Contus's two-cubit pole swinging in his tunic. He smiled. "I will take communion."

Paleos unfastened his breeches and let them drop to the deck. His penis was astonishingly large, given the man's short, bulky frame.

Chrysion said, "You can use any of the catamites for your pleasure, and that will constitute communion."

Paleos looked him right in the eye and responded. "I have lusted for you since you first set foot on this ship."

Chrysion held up a finger in protest. "I am reserved for Contus. You would have to share me."

"Then so shall it be."

Contus filled his lover with his immense, powerful cock, then lay down to allow Paleos entry. The helmsman entered with considerable effort, and Chrysion cried out in pain.

"Have I hurt you, son?" Paleos put a reassuring paw on the boy's back.

Chrysion nodded. "It is only temporary. It will soon become joy. Press on."

And in that way, Paleos was indoctrinated into the Priapic Brotherhood. He ate of Chrysion's seed and then drank from the large bucket that filled with Contus's and his semen. They passed the bucket around.

The chanter was well-endowed, but the piper was tiny. With Chrysion's guidance, Paleos passed along the communion to those two. The piper put the chanter's "flute" in his mouth, and Paleos deposited his issue in the piper.

Ibrahim, a naturally gifted orator, stood on the prow and proclaimed. "We are free citizens. We are a church. Let us commandeer this ship and make for the Hellespont! First by water, then by land."

The crowd cheered. The men untied the ship and steered it out of the harbor under the massive legs of the Colossus. The vessel would be apprehended in open waters if they went straight across the bay to the nearest port. They decided to land at Physkos and follow the Roman roads to Lampsacus in the Hellespont.

In Physkos, Ibrahim negotiated the sale of the vessel to a local merchant.

CHAPTER 6

In each city or village they passed, the men took communion and shared the potent effluence with the local farmers. In this way, they found protection in each town they passed, and the cult of Priapous grew.

Farmers and merchants all wished to take communion, thereby increasing their crops and the value of their wares. Arriving in a town by nightfall, Ibrahim negotiated the barns and boarding houses for all the escaped slaves with the promise of bountiful crops by dawn. Indeed, the men took communion and scattered the remainder over the vines, roots, and trees that grew there. When the farmers saw the miracle of the holy seed, they converted immediately. In this way, the Temple of Priapous found new members throughout Ionia and Aeolis.

As the men brought the good news, so, too, did the Roman consuls learn of the new religion forming, worshipping a living god. This new religion was a threat to their power and status. As the cult moved closer to Lampsacus, the Empire gathered forces to take siege at Lampsacus when the followers of Priapous arrived.

The two hundred men had grown to five hundred when they arrived at the fortified city of Smyrna, a week's journey from Lampsacus. Two towering hunks of muscle stood watch at the gate when they approached. They were immovable and spoke not when spoken to.

Ibrahim did his best to speak sense into their heads, but they were as still as stone. A voice called down from the parapet above.

"You shall never find peaceful conversation with these warriors. Their minds follow a program after many years of training. Beware, they are dangerous."

Ibrahim called up to the man. "Perhaps you can help us gain entrance, for the night is near, and we have much good news to share with the fine people of Smyrna."

The man descended and opened a small window in the massive drawbridge. He whispered to avoid the guards from overhearing. "There is an entrance used only by merchants and vendors. It is a thousand cubits to the west." He pointed to a distant corner of the wall.

"Knock first three, then one, then three again. In that manner, you shall gain entrance, even though your numbers may be great."

Inside the great city's walls, the former slaves marveled at the splendor of the great marketplace. There were tens of thousands living here, rivaling anything Chrysion or Contus had seen. Not even Istambolia was so magnificent. The five hundred acolytes sat in the syntagma, or town square, while the three leaders searched for farmers with whom to bargain. They wandered the narrow streets, seeing no sign of fields or flowers.

Contus stopped a gentleman in the street. "Where are the farms?"

The man laughed. "This is a town of seafaring merchants. We get our meat, vegetables, milk, and eggs from vendors, and we deal in gold, silver, and lead." He held up three coins to illustrate.

Ibrahim stepped in. "Here, put your three coins in this pot, and they will multiply."

The man named Jonah laughed. "I'm no fool. You'll run off with the jar and my money."

"No, sir," said Ibrahim, "You will hold the jar. I promise you will only gain from this."

The man took the jar, dropped in the coins, and covered the pot with a lid.

"Now shake it a few times." He did as he was told. Upon opening the jar, he gasped, for his money had doubled. "How is this done?"

Ibrahim gestured to Contus. "He is a minor god, and his cock issues magic seed that brings plenty."

Contus lifted his tunic to show the gargantuan cock between his legs.

"What can I do to have more?"

Ibrahim was clever. "You must tell only men who wish to have wealth and plenty. Go forth in the marketplace and spread the word. We meet at sundown in the temple of Mercury."

Jonah agreed to spread the word. He paused. "Is this related to your temple?" He withdrew a necklace, from which was hanging a winged phallus.

Chrysion said, "Where did you get that?"

Jonah smiled. "They came on a fast ship from Physkos and are good luck charms for crops, cattle, fertility, and maritime commerce."

Ibrahim scoured the marketplace, buying every flying phallus he could find, seeing an opportunity to provide a symbol to the newly formed religion. He returned to the town square and distributed them among the former slaves, reserving many more for new recruits.

The amphitheater on the edge of the town lay dormant. It was not yet summer, and the tragedies and comedies were on hiatus. The five hundred men wandered the city streets, spreading the good news of the mighty phallus of Contus Pedalis and giving a winged penis to anyone who agreed to attend the ceremony.

That night, in addition to the five hundred acolytes, several hundred citizens of Smyrna attended communion. At the appointed hour, they disrobed and began the joyful union that transmitted the power of Contus to everyone present. When fellowship ended, there were over seven hundred followers of the faith, consecrated with sperm.

The congregant brought the sperm to the harbor, where they applied it to the prow of each merchant ship. With two hundred residents of Smyrna to spread the news, it would soon become a maritime power to rival Athens or Rome.

CHAPTER 7

The five hundred departed the following day, hoping to reach Lampsacus, the prophesied seat of the religion. They encountered Roman centurions on the path a day's journey south of Lampsacus near the ruins of the ancient kingdom of Troy.

"Ho! Who is this band of travelers? What business have you on the Roman road?"

Ibrahim spoke frankly. "We're followers of Priapus, the god of fertility, abundance, and crops."

The Head Centurion, Marcellus, grabbed Ibrahim and threw him in chains. The other soldiers surrounded as many members of the temple as they could.

Marcellus said, "We have orders from the Emperor himself to end this blasphemous cult. You dare put gods forward before Mercury, Apollo, Jove, or Minerva? You'll end your days in chains."

Ibrahim was undaunted. "Sir, if you but see the miracle of the cock of Contus Pedalis, you may feel its power and be swayed to join us."

"Abandon my post for a false god? I think not!"

The other soldiers began to put the members in chains. Contus stood on a rock and lifted his tunic. "Behold, this cock comes from Mount Olympus itself. Can you not see its god-like stature?"

Marcellus paused. The other soldiers grew slack-jawed.

Ibrahim added, "One drop of his sperm will make you a rich man. You'll have no need to serve an Emperor for small coins when you can have gold."

The sight of such an enormous cock was powerful. The soldiers began whispering amongst themselves.

Marcellus said, "How does it work?"

Contus stepped forward. "Put a hand here, and you'll feel the power of my cock."

Marcellus touched the mighty phallus and trembled. "It's true! There's power here. How may I know it?"

Seven of the thirty centurions were large enough to enter the second chamber. Marcellus was the largest, so he went first. One by one, they spilled their seed inside Chrysion and drank of his semen, adding their own to that of Contus. The other twenty-three soldiers reluctantly bent at the waist and allowed the top members of their legion to penetrate them and share in communion. Contus emptied his bowels of the holy seed into Marcellus's helmet, and all shared the nourishing brew. Although it was only one helmet, miraculously, it provided enough sustenance for the five hundred and thirty men.

Drunk on sperm, Marcellus swooned and sat on a stone. "I feel better than I have since my youth. Truly there is power in the sperm."

Ibrahim was still in cuffs. "Will you release me, kind sir?"

Marcellus produced a key and unchained his prisoner. "I will accompany you to Lampsacus, where several hundred soldiers are waiting to capture you."

So the raggedy band of sperm-eaters marched alongside their guardian Roman soldiers, reaching the outskirts of Lampsacus before sundown the next day.

Until the conversion at Smyrna, Contus's spiritual power had gone unnoticed by the gods on Mount Olympus. After so many men switched alliances to their new god, the god of cock, Zeus and his court were greatly upset. They had put a favorable wind to the backs of the Centurions, meddling in human affairs to correct the perceived imbalance. Still, the Centurions fell in worship of the almighty phallus. So, Diana filled her quiver with charmed arrows and stalked the great Contus Pedalis, now called Priapus, determined to end his reign. The day Contus marched into Lampsacus, the townspeople flocked to his side.

"The day of prophecy is here! The day we make a god of a man." The town's women prepared a mighty feast to feed the hungry horde. After the slaves and soldiers ate their fill, they gathered in the great temple that the townsmen had erected shortly after Contus's birth in expectation of the prophecy that one day he would return to found a mighty church.

Many men had taken the sacred communion already, and the orgy began with little planning. Contus mounted his lover, filling him to the ribs with his massive cock. Chrysion moaned with delight. "Contus, your love is greater than even your cock. I feel it in me, on me, and around me."

Contus kissed his young lover on the lips. "I will love you for eternity."

Centurions with giant cocks plowed men with mere nipples between their legs. Everywhere, seed spilled. Basins caught the holy communion, and the men shared it.

Chrysion felt the immense power of his lover in his belly. His waves of orgasm stroked the mighty cock of Priapus. When he spilled his seed, Chrysion fed it to his lover. When he came a second time, Contus threw his head behind him and roared, flooding Chrysion with more semen than ever before. It was so much it ran from his bottom past the colossal cock and into the basin below.

"I love you, Chrysion."

"And I love you."

CHAPTER 8

These vows of love were the last words of Contus and Chrysion. As they pledged their love, Diana, hiding in the rafters, released an arrow, piercing Contus through the waist and passing into the belly of Chrysion. At that moment, Contus turned to wood. His cock was the trunk of a mighty fig tree, and Chrysion became the fruit. The congregation wept and gnashed their teeth, seeing their god turned to wood and his beloved vessel turned to figs.

They passed the last bowl of his communion and poured the remainder on the fallow fields of grain that hadn't produced a surplus in many years. That year, the harvest was elevenfold what it had been years prior.

Diana's arrow only killed the mortal flesh of the two lovers. Their legacy, the holy communion of sacred sperm, lived in the towns where it was first spilled and spread to many towns far and wide. At Pompeii in Magna Grecia, the cult took hold so completely that it angered even Vulcan, who so rarely paid attention to the affairs of man. He destroyed that city and many surrounding towns to wipe out the cult of Priapus. But it has endured, taking many forms.

It is said that any thief stealing from a field guarded by a wooden carving of Priapus will feel his wrath. Such a thief, if young, Priapus will penetrate in the night. If the thief has a beard, Priapus will force himself into the man's mouth, thereby choking him to death. Even women who steal will feel their wombs ripped apart by the almighty cock that only Chrysion could endure. If the thief steals figs, they will surely die, for they are taking Chrysion from Contus. The wrath will be tenfold.

Just as Contus protected the slaves aboard the ship, oarsmen and sailors alike wear the phallus around their neck and eat figs before setting out to sea. The old gods grew weak, but Priapus lived on. When the son of the Hebrew God spread his gospel, it was accepted by many. The followers of Priapus saw no reason to give up the living god who had blessed their crops, so they welcomed the son into their hearts but kept their cocks and holes in service to their erect, wooden god.

The cult of Priapus thrived and spread to many men

around the known world. The fig tree at Lampsacus still bears fruit all year long. The fruit of the tree has the unusual property of shrinking the penis of any man who eats it, making them a perfect vessel for communion. Whomsoever wears a branch from the tree in his belt will see his cock grow enough to reach the second chamber. For that reason, the tree remains hidden in a cloister for protection. The guardians of the tree will instruct any visitors on the proper means of conducting communion. As a result, many Priapic temples have appeared in cities of the old world and the new.

So ends the tale of Chrysion Bipenna and Contus Pedalis, no longer mortal men but deities.

ABOUT THE AUTHOR

Peter Schutes is a fictional character. He was modeled after the gay pulp fiction authors of the 1970s and 1980s. His creator often wondered who the men were who wrote these books, and so he created Peter to satisfy his curiosity.

Peter was born in 1896 to a wealthy New England family. He carried a massive burden his whole life: he had a gigantic penis. His sex life was defined by the men who worshipped him.

Peter led a tempestuous life, documented in the fictional masterpiece "The Autobiography of Peter Schutes." To learn more about this prolific and prodigious author, we recommend reading his immortal tale of life with too much of a good thing.

OTHER BOOKS FROM PETER SCHUTES PUBLISHING

E-books and Paperbacks (as noted)

The Able Seaman

The Anaconda Copper

The Autobiography of Peter Schutes*

Backwoods Delivery

Big Bodies of All Sizes*

Big Hole River*

Bobbing Buoys and Salty Seamen*

Bunkhouse Buddies*

The Butt Baby*

Cloistered

Confessions of a Rodeo Clown*

Dark as a Dungeon*

Demonic Deception *aka* Deceived, Cursed & Blessed

Desert Island Daddies

The Expectant Member

Firehouse Lovers

The Fish

Five Erotic Tales*

Hercules and Lippos

Hobo Honey

Hot Blue Collars*

Hotshot

Logger's Delight

Muscle Bottom*

Panama Heat

Satanic Seductions*

Satan's Sissy Boy

The Slaves of Rome*

The Thigh Baby

Under the Boardwalk

World's Biggest

Coming Soon

Backwoods Delivery - The Complete Daddy's Boy Series

Like the Greeks Do*

Higher Education*

Hoboes, Hustlers, and Jailbirds*

Small Cockpits and Big Hangars*

Tales of Two Daddies*

*Available as Paperbacks